"Where did Morris go?" Boris said.

"D...

Bo... **DATE DUE** ...you tell us not to go over by the old red tractor, Kikki?"

"Yeah! Why?"

Boris shook his head in shame. "That's right where he's headed."

The three of us took off running toward the tractor.

"Keep your eyes on him," I told Boris.

Boris was leading the pack. Doris was right behind him and I took up the back position. We were running full speed ahead. Then, without warning, Boris stopped still in his tracks. Since Doris was following too close, her face smacked into his rump.

"What's the matter, Boris?" I asked.

"He's gone. He just disappeared. I could see his ears above the grass and part of his face, then all of a sudden—he just disappeared!"

Books by Nikki Wallace:
Stubby and the Puppy Pack

Books by Bill Wallace:
Red Dog
The Backward Bird Dog
Beauty
The Biggest Klutz in Fifth Grade
Blackwater Swamp
Buffalo Gal
The Christmas Spurs
Coyote Autumn
Danger in Quicksand Swamp
Danger on Panther Peak
[Original title: Shadow on the Snow]
A Dog Called Kitty
Eye of the Great Bear
Ferret in the Bedroom, Lizards in the Fridge
The Final Freedom
Journey into Terror
Never Say Quit
Red Dog
Snot Stew
Totally Disgusting!
Trapped in Death Cave
True Friends
Upchuck and the Rotten Willy
Upchuck and the Rotten Willy: The Great Escape
Watchdog and the Coyotes

Books by Carol and Bill Wallace:
The Flying Flea, Callie, and Me
That Furball Puppy and Me
Chomps, Flea and Gray Cat (That's Me!)
Bub Moose

Available from SIMON & SCHUSTER

Nikki Wallace

Stubby and the Puppy Pack to the Rescue

Illustrated by John Steven Gurney

ALADDIN PAPERBACKS

NEW YORK   LONDON   TORONTO   SYDNEY   SINGAPORE

First Aladdin Paperbacks edition July 2003
Text copyright © 2002 by Nikki Wallace
Illustrations copyright © 2002 by John Steven Gurney

ALADDIN PAPERBACKS
An imprint of Simon & Schuster Children's Publishing Division
1230 Avenue of the Americas, New York, NY 10020

Also available in a Simon & Schuster Books for Young Readers hardcover edition.
The text of this book was set in Trump Mediaeval.

Printed in the United States of America
2 4 6 8 10 9 7 5 3 1

The Library of Congress has cataloged the hardcover edition as follows:
Wallace, Nikki.
Stubby and the Puppy Pack to the rescue / by Nikki Wallace ; illustrated by John Steven Gurney.
p. cm.
Summary: Kikki the cat and her dog and cat friends play together and protect each other from dangers in their neighborhood.
ISBN 0-7434-2694-0
[1.Cats—Fiction. 2. Dogs—Fiction. 3. Friendship—Fiction.]
I. Gurney, John Steven, ill. II. Title.
II. PZ7.W15876 Su 2002   [Fic]—dc21   2001057758

ISBN 0-7434-2695-9 (Aladdin pbk.)

To my in-laws, with love . . .
Virginia and Charlie Aldridge
and
Alice and Jim Moore

CHAPTER 1

CRUNCH . . . CRUNCH, CRUNCH.

I stayed perfectly still and low to the ground. Breathing as quietly as I could, I listened. The crunching stopped and all I could hear was my heartbeat pounding inside my head. When I turned toward the noise, it started up again.

CRUNCH, CRUNCH . . . CRUNCH.

This time it was louder, moving closer. I burrowed deeper into the red and gold leaves that were piled high under the giant oak tree. Muscles tensed, I was ready to run if I had to. I peered up through the leaves. A large figure loomed above me. A huge wrinkled face pushed aside the dry, crunchy leaves as it inched its way closer and closer. Finally I could feel warm dog breath on my cheek. I couldn't move. My body froze as his nose pressed into my side. He nudged me.

"Aren't you supposed to run from me?" he asked in a deep rumbly voice.

I shot straight up in the oak tree to the lowest branch. Boris's face wrinkled even more as he frowned up at me.

"I don't understand how this game works, Kikki," he said as he settled down in the pile of leaves. "I thought you were supposed to run from me and I was supposed to chase you. If I tagged you before you got to the porch, then you were It. What's wrong? Did you forget how to play?"

I took a deep breath to relax myself, then jumped to the ground. I plopped down in the leaves next to Boris. He was an enormous dog with the biggest paws I'd ever seen. He called himself a Mastiff, but I called him massive. He said Mastiff was a *breed* of dog. His sister, Doris, was one, too. He told me that the last time he went to the vet, he weighed one hundred and ninety pounds, which was a great deal more than my small cat frame. If I remember, I was only nine pounds the last time the vet weighed me.

"I guess I got scared," I said.

"You know I'm always careful when I play chase with you. Our cat, Charlie, taught me and Doris how to watch where we're going when we play with cats. We don't chase him anymore because he's so old, but we learned how to tag with our noses instead of our feet. What's the big deal anyway? You and I have been playing this game for a couple of months, and you said you weren't scared of me anymore."

I started to tremble again, not because I was scared of Boris, but because I thought about Max. I could picture his yellow teeth and smell his stinky breath as if he were there.

Before Boris, Doris, and Morris had moved in, my best cat friend, Teebo, lived in their house. One day Teebo and I had decided to take a shortcut through Max's yard to get to the meadow. Teebo made it to the other side. He yelled at me to hurry. I had just started

across the yard when Max, the meanest Dober-
man in the world, came roaring and snarling at
me from his doghouse. I ran! But not fast
enough. Max bit down on my tail and began to
pull. He growled and snarled and shook it back
and forth. I flew back and forth, too. Fortunately, Teebo was there. He jumped on Max's
back and started clawing at his nose. I pulled
away and crawled under the fence to Teebo's
yard. I was safe, but most of my tail was left
behind. That's when Teebo gave me the nick-
name Stubby. Since Teebo was my best friend
and he saved me from Max, he was the only
one I would let call me Stubby. That is until I
made friends with the Puppy Pack. Mostly,
they call me Kikki, but every once in a while
they call call me Stubby.

"Kikki?"
Boris was so close, his breath shook my
whiskers. I blinked, chasing away the nasty
pictures of Max.
"Kikki?" Boris repeated. "Are you okay?"
"To be honest, it's not you that scares me.
When you stood there . . . when you kept get-

ting closer . . . you reminded me of Max. For some reason I got that helpless feeling again."

Boris put his nose in my face. I laughed as he stared at me. He was so close his eyes crossed.

"Don't you worry, Stubby. Remember the first day we met—the time you fell out of the tree into Max's yard? We crashed through the fence to save you. We knew Max was mean and nasty because he talked to us through the fence and told us how tough he was. He told us not to mess with him. You know we'll always take care of you, so you don't have to worry about Max anymore. We're here to protect you. In fact, if this game makes you nervous, we don't have to play it ever again. There are other games we can play."

He gave me a love nudge with his nose. I leaped onto his back and wrapped my paws, as far as I could reach, around his thick neck. "Thanks, that means a lot to me. I think I'll be okay, I just need to do something else right now."

Boris stood up with me still clinging to his neck. "Let's find Doris and Morris and see what they want to do. Maybe we could meet the nice lady who gives you milk. We've lived here a couple of months now, and we've never left our yard."

Doris and Morris were still hiding. Doris was Boris's sister. She was big, but not quite as big as Boris. Their faces were both droopy and wrinkled. Boris had tan fur and Doris had dark brown fur with tan spots. Morris looked a lot different from either of them. His breed was called Scottie. He was bigger than I, but still a lot smaller than Boris and Doris. His fur was white and his ears looked like they belonged to a jackrabbit. I figured Doris was probably behind the rocks that surrounded the garden pond. That was really the only place she and Boris could hide. It was the only thing in the yard big enough to cover their enormous bodies. Well, except for the shed and their doghouses. But she usually hid behind the rocks.

"Over there." I used my paws to guide him.

He trotted toward the pond. Doris was lying down, but her hind end stuck up behind the red rocks that surrounded the murky water.

"See her bottom?" I whispered. "She's back

there behind the rocks by the fence. Let's sneak up on her."

Doris was too busy peeking around the other side of the rocks to notice us creeping up behind her. I flattened myself against Boris's back as he crouched low to the ground. He inched closer and closer. I could feel the rumble that started deep in his throat. First a low growl, then, in his deepest voice . . .

"WOOF, WOOF, WOOF."

Doris didn't turn around. She tucked her tail and ran to the back door of her People's house. She curled herself in a ball and whimpered. Boris dropped to the ground. He was laughing so hard that I bounced right off his back. Of course, if I hadn't been so tickled I might have kept my perch on his neck. For such a large dog, Doris sure got spooked awfully easy.

When she realized it was Boris and I who had scared her, she trotted over to us. "You two frightened me. I was running so fast, I thought I was going to knock the door to the house down. I looked pretty silly, huh?" Her tail waved back and forth.

I glanced around the yard, trying to find my

other friend. Being smaller than Boris and Doris, he had a few more places he could hide. Not many, though, because the grass and garden had dried up and turned brown. There was no tall monkey grass to hide behind or big green bushes. I smiled as I thought of Teebo and how he used to hide in the monkey grass. I could always find him when he hid there because his tail would twitch and move the long green blades. I missed him but knew he would really like my new friends. I swallowed the lump that formed in my throat.

It had been several months since Teebo moved away, but it still made me sad to think of him. He'd been the best friend any cat could have. We had fun together. When he moved, I never thought I would have another buddy. There weren't many nice cats in my neighborhood, and I was scared of dogs. Well . . . that was until I met Morris, Doris, and Boris. They had scared me at first, but when they saved me from Max, I knew we could be lifelong friends.

* * *

"Kikki?"

The sound of my name snapped me from my memory of Teebo. Doris towered above me, wagging her tail.

"Oh, hi." My fur rippled. "Let's find Morris and play something else."

Doris headed around the silver shed. Boris and I started for the back door. The porch had been redone since Teebo moved out. My new friends' People had worked on it every weekend for a whole month. They used new wood and made it a lot bigger. It looked really nice. It was decorated with a big pot that was full of white and purple mums. A small scarecrow sat on a bale of hay near the back door, and pumpkins were scattered around the bottom of the bale. As we got closer to the porch, I saw two white tips sticking up next to the scarecrow.

"Hey, Boris, I think I see him. Over there behind the hay." The white tips were definitely Scottie ears. Morris's ears stood up tall and pointy on his head. They didn't lie down like Boris's and Doris's.

"Let's try to sneak up on him like we did Doris," I whispered.

Once more Boris crouched low to the ground. We quietly crept around the side of the hay. I could feel that rumble starting in Boris's throat again, but it was different this time.

"Woofff . . . AHHHCHOOO!"

Morris turned on us and started to giggle. "He's allergic to hay. Ha ha! You didn't scare me. You'll never be able to sneak up and scare me."

Boris sneezed about five more times. When he was through, Doris trotted up beside us.

Morris gave one more chuckle. "I was the last one to be caught. Now you guys go hide." Boris turned, looked up at me, and gave a wink. "No, I'm tired of playing hide-and-go-seek. Let's play tug-of-war."

Boris ran over and scrounged through several pieces of rope. He finally settled for a fairly new wiggy. Wiggy was what they called their chewy toy. It looked like a colorful rope with both ends frayed. Morris chewed up most of them. With his head held high, Boris paraded back and forth in front of Doris until she finally grabbed one end of it. They tugged and pulled and yanked and growled. Huge muscles rippled. The dogs were so big and powerful they seemed to shake the ground. Boris gave one mighty shake and pulled it away from Doris. When he did, Morris jumped in and took her spot. Boris flipped the wiggy and Morris from side to side. Morris refused to let go. With one last powerful jerk, Boris flung Morris across the yard.

"Okay, that's enough. Why don't we go visit Fern?" Boris barked.

Morris got up and shook the grass off. All bristly, he strutted back on stiff legs. "I'm not ready to go to Fern's. Just because you're big, Boris, I'm not afraid of you. I'm not scared to play tug-of-war."

"I like Boris's idea," Doris agreed, wagging her tail. "Fern sounds like the next-door neighbor we used to have. She liked to feed us scraps of meat. The fence was made of chain link, so sometimes she would reach her fingers through it and scratch behind our ears."

"I'll go get Charlie," I said. "He can teach me how to open the fence, and maybe he'll want to go, too."

Morris held his nose and the wiggy high in the air. He trotted over to his food bowl beside the fence to lie down and pout. Then he started gnawing on his food bowl.

Doris saw the frown on my face. "He chews on things when he gets nervous or mad."

I jumped up on the porch where Charlie was resting in the sun.

"Hey, Charlie, can you help us?" I asked.

Charlie stretched his legs. "Sure, Kikki, what's the problem?"

"Well, it's not really a problem, but do you remember when you said that one day you would teach me how to open the gate?"

"Yeah," Charlie said with a slight grin on his face. "If it's anything like the gate at our old place, the dogs do most of the work. All you have to do is catch the latch." His whiskers twitched a little bit.

"I'm ready to learn," I said.

I think Charlie liked to teach me all his tricks. One time he said I reminded him of himself when he was younger.

I ran ahead of Charlie. Doris and Boris were already standing near the old wooden gate. I could hear Boris mumbling something about how this fence was a little different from the one at their old house.

"Morris, why don't you come help us out. You're pretty good at getting a latch up," Charlie complimented him.

Charlie hopped up on the post, above where the black metal thing was.

"Come on, Kikki. It's big enough for both of us up here."

Careful not to knock Charlie over, I jumped up beside him. Holding with the claws of his right paw, Charlie leaned over and reached as far as he could with his left. His claws were about an inch or so above the flat plate on the black metal thing.

"You try it, Kikki. Maybe your arms are longer than mine."

Making sure my claws had a good grip in the wooden post, I leaned down like Charlie had done. I came up just a little short, too.

"That's okay, Kikki," Charlie said with a flip of his tail. He looked around. Morris was still in the corner of the yard with the wiggy in his mouth.

"Morris," Charlie meowed, "we really need your help. We can't open the gate without you."

Charlie turned to me and whispered, "Morris is insecure around the big dogs sometimes. That's why he's pouting. Since he's smaller, he doesn't feel like he can do as much as they can. It helps to praise him when he does a good job. It makes him feel better about himself."

"Ready, Morris?" Charlie asked when Morris got to the gate.

Morris frowned. "It doesn't look like the same latch that was on our gate."

"It's not," Charlie agreed. "Our latch was a little plate on the side. This one is on the top. See where the metal sticks out a little? That's what you need to go for."

Morris's long tail wagged back and forth. "Okay. I'm ready," he yapped. Ears straight up and pointed, he listened for Charlie and waited for his cue.

"Now!"

Morris bounced up and down about three times. Each time his nose came closer to the latch that held the gate closed. On the fourth jump, he hit the black metal handle with his nose. Charlie reached out and caught the latch just as it flipped up. He held it open with his paw.

"That's the only part you really have to do," Charlie said with a flip of his tail. "I'll let you try it next. You will be working really close to Morris's nose. Just be sure you don't get a claw hung in his snout when you grab the latch."

Charlie let go and the latch clicked shut. He stepped aside so I could hold on to the post and hang over the side. When I was ready, he meowed, "Now, Morris."

Again Morris hopped and bounced against the gate. It took me two tries, but I finally caught the latch.

"Okay, Morris," Charlie said, "now you've got to use your paw to pull the gate toward you."

"I figured that out," Morris scoffed. "This part is just like the gate at our other house."

Charlie nodded his head patiently. "Boris you stand by, and when he gets it open a little, put your nose in the crack and then push it open. When you come back, Kikki, all you have to do is push it shut. Just make sure you shove it all the way until you hear it catch."

"Let me close it, then we'll practice opening it," I said.

Charlie jumped down. "You guys be careful and have fun. I'm going back to finish my nap."

We all assured him that we'd be careful.

"Now!" I yelled down to Morris.

He did his bouncy thing and lifted the latch. I grabbed for it but missed.

"Catch it this time," Morris said as he hit the latch again.

I was proud when I caught it.

"Let's go!" Doris said with her tongue hanging out one side of her mouth.

We all charged to the front yard, and they followed me toward Fern's house.

CHAPTER 2

I crossed the street to my house. The three dogs followed close behind me with their tongues sticking out the sides of their mouths. Doris's tongue was hanging out the most. For some reason, she always had it flopping out one side or the other. I guess she just had too much tongue.

"This is my house," I said. "My family isn't home right now, but I want you to meet them sometime. They are the best family a cat could ever have."

I showed them the backyard. It wasn't as big as their yard, but it was just as nice. Carol, my Mama People, had a hammock tied between two big oak trees. She left it up all year. Sometimes, even when we had cold weather, she liked to sit in it and watch the birds. There were three large birdhouses in the yard and several hummingbird feeders.

"When Carol isn't watching, I like to chase the little fluttery creatures. I never hurt them, but it's fun to watch the whole bunch fly away when I charge at the feeder. One time Carol caught me darting after them. I thought she was busy reading, but I was wrong. Quietly she rolled up her magazine and chased me with it. She swatted at me, yelling, 'Don't you eat my birds, you little rascal.' Now I only chase them when I'm positive she isn't watching me. She's never spanked me, but I'm always scared when I see that wad of paper swinging down toward my backside."

"Just be glad she didn't hit you," Morris mumbled. "That really hurts."

Boris trotted between us. "When do we go meet your friend?" he asked.

"We'd better head to Fern's now or we might miss her. Come on!"

"I don't want to go," Morris grumped. "Let's stay here."

I walked around to the side yard and jumped over the fence. I trotted a little way up the street. It took me a while to realize the dogs weren't behind me. When I looked back at my yard, the three of them were sitting there with silly looks on their faces.

"Did you forget that we can't jump a fence like you?" Boris asked.

I ducked my head. "Yeah, I guess I did. I'll wait for you guys on the other side near the gate."

I watched them for a few seconds. They were taking their time, sniffing Carol's flowers as they headed for the open gate. I walked along the cement blocks that bordered our front flower bed. I froze when I heard the clanking sound of a dog collar behind me. I turned to see Max trotting along beside his People. They did not have a leash on him, and they were too busy talking to pay much attention to what Max was doing. Since he hadn't spotted me, I sneaked into the bushes beside the front porch. I guess my movement caught his attention, because I could hear him run up to the bush I was hiding under. His long snout whiffed the plants.

"Come here, little kitty. I know you're in there, I saw you. You can't hide from me."

His owners were still walking and talking, paying no mind to what Max was doing. I held my breath, trying to be as still as I could.

Where were my dogs? I thought to myself. *They must have stopped to look at something, or else they would have already chased Max away.*

"Aw, there you are."

I backed farther into the corner as Max glared down at me. Slobbers dripped from the sides of his mouth when he licked his lips.

"I knew I'd catch you away from your bodyguards. I've waited patiently for this, and now I've got you!"

His lip curled up on one side as he pushed his way farther into the bush. I shoved back, flattening myself against the porch. There was nowhere to go. With a snarl, Max opened his mouth. White fangs glistened, then snapped shut. I closed my eyes. How he missed me, I don't know. His sharp teeth flashed again. I could almost feel his long incisors piercing my skin. Instead, there was a large *clunk* sound, then a whimper. I opened my eyes. A large paw pinned Max's head to the ground. The weight of it shoved the side of his face into the soft soil. Max spit and coughed as Boris increased the pressure.

"What did we tell you about messing with our cat?" Boris growled.

Morris nipped at Max's rump while Doris stood nearby, ready to pounce if she was needed.

"I . . . I . . . was just p-p-playing with her," Max stammered. "I wasn't going to hurt her, honest."

Boris gave Max one last shove into the dirt.

"Get your dirty self out of here and don't let me see you again," Boris growled.

Max jumped up and raced toward his owners, who were way down the street and still ignoring the world around them. Head low and tail tucked, Max managed to squeeze himself between his Mama and Daddy.

I took in a deep breath. "What took you guys so long? Max almost got me."

I felt sick to my stomach and my head was spinning.

"I think she's going to pass out," Doris said.

When I woke up, my friends were waving their tails back and forth over my face to give me some air. I stood up and gave myself a little shake.

Doris stood in front of me with her head cocked to one side. "Maybe we should just go home now."

"No, I'm fine. I want you to meet Fern. I'll just stick close to you guys and everything should be okay. From the looks of it, I don't think Max will be back for a while anyway." I managed to grin up at them.

We started toward Fern's house. We crossed the street to the Williamses' yard, and I showed them the garden where Teebo and I used to play.

"In the summer this garden has huge flowers growing in it. They're really tall and pretty. Teebo and I liked to chase worms and grasshoppers that wiggled in the cool, damp dirt under them."

Boris sniffed the edge of the garden. Mrs. Williams had planted a few mums, but mostly the earth was covered with wood chips. Boris stopped and stared intently at one of the mum plants. He shoved at the dirt with his nose. We watched him closely as he pushed his head deeper under the plant. His tail wagged back and forth.

"Hi," he barked. "Whatcha doin' under there?"

Boris was so big, I didn't even have to scrunch down to walk under him. I just strolled up and stood between his front legs to see who he was talking to. There was a tiny white fuzz ball hiding beneath the mum.

"White Kitty, is that you?" I asked.

The little cat had blue eyes. They were so big around, I could hardly see much else.

"Yes, Kikki, it's me," a tiny voice meowed back.

I wasn't good friends with White Kitty, but I had played chase with him once or twice before. He looked really nervous.

"What's wrong? Did the big dogs scare you? They're sweet and they like cats."

"I'm not scared of the dogs," White Kitty said, trembling.

"Well, then, why are you so—"

Before I could finish my sentence, fear swept over me. I remembered the first time I met White Kitty. It was in the tree house—Kylie's tree house. My tail puffed—just a little. Without turning around, I could feel Kylie's presence. I could smell the stinky perfume she poured all over herself. I turned to warn Boris, Doris, and Morris, but it was too late. They had already met her face to face. She was already there! I scampered in and huddled next to White Kitty underneath the mum bush. The three dogs were sitting beside one another, facing Kylie. It was quiet for a long time and then . . .

"Woof!" Boris wagged his tail to say hello.

"Ahhhh!" Kylie screamed back at him.

"Woof!" Doris said hi, too.

Once again Kylie screamed. She yelled at the top of her lungs. It was as if she wanted to see if they would bark at her again.

Boris took a small step toward Kylie and sat back down.

"Woof, woof, woof!" he barked. "Do you want to play with us?"

Kylie didn't bother screaming this time. She

just turned and ran. Even when she fell over her big shoes, she got right back up and raced to her house. I watched as Kylie ran in and slammed the door behind her. Her screams pierced the cool air even though they were coming from inside her house. We all flattened our ears against our heads.

"That child is scary," Boris said. "I'm a big dog and she scared me."

"I'm sorry." I shrugged my ears. "I forgot to warn you about Kylie. She is mean. Her favorite thing is zipping cats and kittens up in her pink backpack and hauling them up to her tree house. I can't tell you the rest right now because it bothers me to talk about it."

Boris looked around. "What happened to White Kitty?"

"Well, Kylie took off in one direction and White Kitty the other," I said. *Really, I think he was more scared of Kylie than the big dogs.*

"Have you been up in her tree house?" Morris asked.

"Yeah, she caught Teebo and me once." A chill rippled the fur down my back. "Let me just say, it was not a fun experience. I guess

she's scared of you three, but be careful when you see her anyway. I wouldn't want any of my enemies, much less my friends, to be taken up to the tree house."

"Let's go meet Fern," Boris barked.

"This is it, right here," I meowed. "Poor Fern has to live right next door to Kylie."

We trotted over to her porch. I stretched my front paws up on the screen door. I could see her in the kitchen. She was wearing a long blue robe and her little white slippers were peeking out of the bottom. I guess she saw us coming, because I only had to shake the screen once before she came to the door.

"Remember," I coached. "Be really nice. Sit here and wait to see if she offers you anything. I don't want her to be scared of you."

Fern hesitated a moment before she opened the door and came out.

Boris and Doris sat quietly near the steps while Morris stood back at the very edge of the porch.

"Hi, Kikki. Who are your friends?" Fern reached down and scratched Doris behind the ears.

Then she walked over and sat on her porch swing. Like always, she patted the blanket next to her. That was where I usually sat. Before I had a chance to move, I noticed the look in Boris's eyes. His body shook with excitement.

"No, Boris, don't do it!" Doris yelled.

But it was too late. His enormous body thundered across the porch. Fern saw him coming. Her eyes wide, she braced herself. Boards shook beneath my feet as Boris leaped for the spot where he thought Fern wanted him to sit on the swing. Fern's feet flailed in the air as she grabbed for the side rail to keep herself from falling out. Boris licked her face.

"Whoa, big boy. Get down." She laughed.

"Boris! You know better than that. Kikki told you to be nice, so get down off the swing. Now!" Doris scolded.

Boris's jowls drooped as he flopped out of the swing. Fern got up and straightened the blanket she had spread out on the seat. She puffed her hair with her hands and fixed her glasses so she could see.

"Let's try this again," she said, turning to sit down.

The minute her bottom touched the swing, Boris's tail started flopping back and forth. She leaned over and patted the porch beside her shoes. Boris and Doris sat next to Fern's feet.

"Come on, Kikki," Fern said. "You can get up here. But your friends, well, they're a bit too big to crawl up here with me."

Morris was still sitting at the edge of the porch. Fern reached over and grabbed my special bowl off the window ledge. She reached into her pocket and pulled out a bag full of turkey scraps.

"Here you go, Kikki. I'll give you the first bite." Fern smiled as she tore off a piece of turkey and put it in the bowl in front of me.

Fern gave both Boris and Doris a big piece. They gulped it down and waited for another bite.

"Hey, little doggie, don't you want a bite?" Fern held a piece of turkey out for Morris.

For a second Morris looked away. Then he turned toward her. His ears were back and he held his head low. He crept closer to Fern. She stretched her hand out as far as she could. Cautiously Morris reached out and grabbed the turkey with his teeth then ran back to his place near the stairs.

Doris looked up at me. "He's pretty scared of strangers. Well, come to think of it, he's scared of just about everyone except our People, Mandy and Todd."

"Why?" I asked.

"I'll tell you later. When we're alone," Doris whispered.

Fern fed us the rest of the turkey. Morris got up to get one more piece, but he took it back to the stairs to eat it.

"We've got some time to take a nap if you want," I said, stretching my feet out on the blanket.

"Sounds good to me." Doris yawned.

Boris nodded his head in agreement. I looked over at Morris. He was lying down, but his eyes never left Fern. The two big dogs nestled their cheeks on Fern's slippers. I could tell they really liked her by the way they snuggled up next to her. She liked them, too. Before Fern began knitting, she leaned over and gave Boris and Doris a good rub behind the ears. We all dozed off.

I woke up when the swing moved. Fern stood up and waddled to the house.

"I've got to go inside now, but you are all welcome to keep napping if you'd like. It was nice to see you, and I hope you come back soon."

I purred for Fern as she reached down to stroke my back. She picked up my bowl and her knitting basket and went inside. Boris and Doris stood at the door wagging their tails.

"I guess we should go home. I don't want Mandy and Todd worrying about us," Doris said.

Boris, Morris, and I followed her down the steps.

Morris stopped suddenly. "I want to explore the neighborhood."

Doris glanced back at him. "We really should get home."

"Just because you're big doesn't mean that you can order me around. I'm going to go explore."

Morris headed off in the opposite direction.

"Just let him go," Doris said. "He'll get over it."

The two big dogs and I continued toward the

house. Suddenly Boris's legs locked. He stopped so quick his nails scratched the concrete.

"Look!" Boris yelled. "It's the dog police. We'd better run."

The big truck rumbled around the corner toward us.

"Get home!" I screamed. "Don't worry about me, I can outrun them. Save yourselves."

Boris and Doris darted for their house. Morris heard the commotion and decided to run home, too. He couldn't quite catch up to Boris and Doris because of his short legs. The tires on the truck screeched to a stop. Two men leaped out. My heart beat extra fast and my legs shook.

"Faster, Morris! Hurry!" I yelled.

The men gained on him. I couldn't let them catch Morris. I flew across the yard so fast that my paws barely touched the dry grass. I zipped between Morris and the man.

"Where'd that cat come from?" one of the men asked.

"I don't know, but catch her," the short one hollered.

I darted in and out of bushes and shrubs. I ran onto porches and laughed as the two men tried to catch me. I was just too fast for them. When I got tired of running around, I glanced back to see where they were. They gave up on me and once again looked for the dogs. I peered toward my friends' house. The gate was closed. They were safe. I sat there for a minute in order to catch my breath. Before I had time to blink, someone scooped me up off the ground.

Was there a third man that I hadn't seen?

Then . . . a familiar smell crinkled my nose. My eyes flashed wide. I didn't have time to struggle. There wasn't even time for my claws to spring out. Suddenly—below me—was the gaping mouth of a pink backpack. The knobs on the zipper shone like pearly teeth ready to eat me.

Which is exactly what it did.

CHAPTER 3

It was dark and scary inside the pink backpack. My sharp ears heard a door slam. Suddenly I felt weightless—like I was falling. My paws felt the impact. It almost buckled my knees. I guess Kylie dropped the bag I was in. I knew exactly what to do when she let me out. If she ever opened this stinkin' backpack, I was gone!

"I've got you now, kitty. Don't worry, I saved you from those big mean dogs. Mama called the pound. I saved your life, so now I will let you be a guest at my tea party."

My stomach turned when she said tea party. I remembered the nasty stuff she called "tea."

It wasn't a pleasant experience. I perked my ears and listened to the slow ripping sound that came from above me. A beam of light flashed into the darkness of the backpack. The metal teeth glimmered as the bag was opened even more. I could see part of a window, but I remained still until I knew it was safe for me to run. Kylie opened it wide.

"Come on out of there, little kitty. It's safe now."

Kylie was sitting on her knees in her tree house. Dirt and grass stained her grungy dress. Her plump fingers glittered with fake diamonds and rubies. Around her neck was a rhinestone necklace with several missing stones. She held one side of the backpack open and peered in at me. Slowly I crawled out. I flattened my ears and stayed low to the ground. I kept both eyes on her until I was far enough away to escape. After leaping to the windowsill, I tried to jump through the opening. But . . . the window was closed. I scratched at the glass, hoping to get it open.

"Where are you going, kitty? You're safe here with me. Daddy put glass in the windows because kitties kept escaping. So I fixed that problem. I'll let you go home after the tea party. We're going to have so much fun!"

I gritted my teeth. Kylie and her dad had fixed up the tree house since the last time I was captured. They painted the walls white. Kylie's name was stenciled in bright pink above the door, and framed pictures of her family were hanging on the walls. Each picture was cocked to one side or the other. Definitely Kylie's doing.

"Which dress do you want? I think this bright yellow will look nice with your coloring," Kylie said, holding up the ugliest dress in the whole pile.

I backed myself into a corner of the room. "Please no. I don't want a dress. I just want to go home," I howled.

Kylie swooped me up in her arms and smiled. I turned my head. I couldn't stand to look at her with the bright green eye shadow and red stuff on her lips. Her unbrushed hair was fuzzy and stood straight up on her head.

"How about some makeup first?" A smirk spread across her face.

She held me close as she sat on the floor near the big mirror that leaned against the wall.

"Purple eye shadow will look really good with the yellow dress," she said as she ran a little brush through the purple powder.

"Now, close your eyes."

I tried once more to wiggle out of her arms, but she just squeezed me tighter. Finally I gave up. I could feel the smooth brush gliding above my eyes. It was awful, but I didn't fight anymore.

"We'll try this new pink color for your cheeks."

I opened my eyes just in time to see an enormous brush headed for the side of my face. The end of it was covered with bright pink powder. I cringed as she brushed the stuff onto my cheeks. The powder was so heavy that it made my whiskers droop.

"Oh, no, I almost forgot to put your shoes on. You need some pretty little heels."

I can't wear those, I thought.

Carol wore them sometimes when she dressed up to go to fancy parties with Bill. Surely there wasn't some crazy person out there making high heels for cats. In her right hand Kylie had a roll of tape. She sat on the floor and tore off a long piece of the tape. She rolled it around her hand five times, with the sticky side facing out.

She grabbed me up in her arms and reached for my back paw. "Okay now, kitty, give me your paw. That's it."

I tried to pull my leg away, but she stuck the gummy strip to my back right paw. Quickly she tore off another long piece of tape, rolled it up, and stuck that on my left foot.

"There you go. See how those work for you," she said as she put me on the ground. "Okay, kitty, walk now."

I tried to run, but my feet stuck to the floor. I had to jerk each foot up—really high—just to get it unstuck. First the left foot, then the right. I almost tipped myself over. I tried to pull off the tape with my teeth, but it was stuck tight.

Kylie laughed. "You look funny. You're wobbling all over the place. Come here and I'll finish you up. Just a couple more things and you'll be dressed for the party."

Kylie reached into her little bag and pulled out several tubes of lipstick. By the time she finished, there were fifteen different colors sitting on the floor. There were many shades of red, pink, orange, and even brown.

"How about red? You're gonna be so pretty when I get through with you. Go like this," Kylie said as she opened her mouth and curled her lips around her teeth. "That way I can get the lipstick where it belongs."

Desperately I squirmed to get away from her. I lowered my head so she couldn't get the lipstick on my face. It didn't work. She just spread the red creamy stuff wherever she could. It started on my forehead, and by the time she finished it was on my cheeks.

"There. Aren't you pretty? Take a look in the mirror." Kylie placed me in front of the big piece of glass.

"What is that?" I howled. I could feel the tingling begin on my back. The tingling I get just before my hair stands on end. I hissed at the hideous creature in the mirror. It looked like a cat, but it had a red line drawn all over it. Purple powder covered most of its forehead.

Back arched, it acted like it wanted to attack me. I hissed at it again, then squirmed away from the creature and out of Kylie's reach.

Oh, no, I realized all at once. *That's me. What has Kylie done to my face? I look so scary I even frighten myself.*

"Now for your perfume. What kind would you like?" Kylie pulled five different bottles out of her bag.

"I'll let you wear my favorite." She picked up a red bottle.

I watched closely as she opened the lid. When she aimed it at my back, I took off. She chased me, trying to hit me with the smelly stuff as I ran circles. For a minute I hid under the table where her dolls were sitting. Kylie peered under the bottom edge of the pink tablecloth. I scooted farther back from her. I watched her feet as she ran around to the other side. I jumped back just out of reach of her dirty little fingers.

Kylie got down on her knees. "Now come on, kitty. This won't hurt. It'll just make you smell real good. Come on out."

The wicked glint in her eye told me to run

away. Run fast. Run far. I froze. There was no way to escape. Nowhere to hide. Kylie grabbed me by the neck . . . aimed . . . fired.

For the next few minutes I coughed and spit. The smell was gross. All I could do was gag.

"See, that didn't hurt. Did it? One last thing and you're ready for tea," she said, pointing to the dolls seated at the table.

My eyes burned. Through tiny slits, all I could see was the bright yellow outline of a doll dress, and then I felt the material on my back.

"Put this arm in first." She lifted my right paw and forced it through a hole in the little dress. "Now, let's try the other arm. Ah, look in the mirror. You are so beautiful. Let's have some tea."

I didn't mean to, but I glanced once more into the mirror. It was worse. No, I was worse. I screeched when I saw myself. Kylie spun me around and shoved me down onto a wooden thing, next to one of the dolls.

"This is your own special seat." The instant Kylie plopped me in the chair and let go, I sprang up and darted under the table. Kylie picked me up and stuck me back in the chair. "You are the guest of honor, so you get to sit here at the end. You also get your tea first."

As she picked up a little pot, I raced to hide near the door. Again, she dragged me back.

Kylie poured my teacup full with one hand, while she pushed me down in the chair with her other. I knew better than to drink the stuff. Teebo and I had tried it before. It was nasty!

"Drink away, kitty. It's good for you. Besides, the rest of us can't drink ours until the guest of honor has had the first sip."

Without taking my eyes off her, I lowered my head to the cup and made slurping noises. Kylie fell for it.

"Good kitty. Now, drink up, my friends," she told the dolls as she lifted her cup.

When Kylie finished drinking her tea, she swooped me up in her arms.

"You can go home now," she said, sliding the window open.

Kylie put me in a really big metal bucket, tied to the end of a rope. Part of the rope hung over a limb of the giant maple tree. On one end of the rope was the bucket with me in it; on

the other end was a huge red brick that rested on the ground. Slowly Kylie pulled the brick end of the rope up. As she did, I got closer to the grass below.

"Oh, no. I forgot to take the dress off you."

All at once I was on my way up again. I wasn't about to go back in there. No way. Before Kylie was able to pull me all the way to the top, I leaped out of the bucket, dress and all.

Finally I was free.

I ran and I ran and I ran. Past the Williamses' house, across the street, and into my own yard.

How can I get out of this dress? Maybe Boris, Doris, and Morris can help.

Quickly I dashed across the street and stopped at the gate. I had to be careful jumping over the fence because I didn't want to get my back feet caught in the bottom of the dress. It would hurt if I did. I stretched my front paws out. For a second I crouched near the gate, trying to get the courage to jump. I took a deep breath and sprang for the fence.

CHAPTER 4

The three dogs waited for me by the porch.

"Oh, my goodness!" Doris laughed. "What happened to you?"

The three of them howled and snorted. Morris was rolling on the grass he was laughing so hard. I glared at them.

When Doris saw my face, she turned to Boris. "That's enough. Kikki is upset."

Boris's expression went blank. He turned to Morris, who was still howling.

"Doris is right. We need to cut it out because we're hurting Kikki's feelings." Boris glared at Morris.

Morris's fur bristled up on his back like the

last time one of the big dogs told him what to do. He kept right on laughing, though. I growled at him. Morris stood in front of me.

"What's that smell?" He giggled.

I took a swat at him. "It's not funny. Kylie captured me when I was trying to save your lives, and all you can do is sit there and laugh at me? If I hadn't darted between you and the dogcatchers, Morris, they would have caught you and taken you to the dog pound. You wouldn't be laughing then, would you?"

Morris's fur bristled even more. He puffed out a breath of air, then went to pout by the fence and his food bowl. The two big dogs were silent as I walked over to them. I lay down with my head on my paws.

"Kikki, I'm sorry we laughed at you." Boris put his nose in my face. "Kylie's not very nice, is she?"

Without looking up, I shook my head. I glanced over at Morris. He was just sitting there with his backside to us, chewing on a piece of rope. He wasn't even going to apologize for being so mean.

"Yeah, I'm sorry, too. I wasn't thinking

about your feelings at first. And it's not that you look that bad, just different." Doris grinned.

I tried to give her a smile, but I was too mad at Morris.

"Kikki, I'm sorry Morris was laughing so hard. He just can't stand it when someone bigger tells him what to do. He probably would have stopped if you had asked him to, but since Boris and I are bigger, he thinks we're being bossy," Doris explained.

I lifted my head. "Remind me next time and we'll try it. Anything's better than having him act that way. It really hurts my feelings, and I'm sure it bothers you, too."

"Come on, Boris, help me get this dress off her," Doris barked.

Doris got on one side of me, Boris on the other.

"Okay, you pull while I try to get my nose between the two pieces of sticky stuff that's holding the dress on," Boris said.

Doris pulled while Boris stuck his cold nose on my back. He nudged at the sticky stuff several times. Every time he did, I could hear the sticky stuff rip a little more and a little more. Finally with one big pull from Doris and one last nudge from Boris, the dress popped open.

"Okay, roll over and we'll pull it off your arms." Doris rolled me with her nose. I ended up on my back, stretching my front paws over my head. Boris clutched the yellow doll dress in his teeth. With one gentle tug, he pulled it off. Sighing, I rolled over on my side. I was finally able to relax. My tape heels were loose, so I was able to pull them off with my teeth.

"Now, how are we going to get that perfume off you?" Doris asked with a wink. "Oh, and don't forget that makeup."

"How about our water bowl?" Boris asked. "Kikki can get her face wet and then rub it on something to get all that paint stuff off."

"Oh, no, I don't think so. There's no way I'm going to get my whole face wet. I hate water. Sure, I like to chase fish and frogs, but when I do that, it's just my feet that get wet, not my face. Well, not on purpose anyway. There is no way I'm going to stick my face in there," I said as I turned my back on them.

"Well, that suits me just fine," Doris huffed.

"I'm not the one that has to go around with a big red line drawn from her forehead to her chin. And I'm not the one that smells so icky."

I dropped to the ground and rubbed my face on the dry grass. I got up and turned to the dogs.

"Did I get it off?"

I could tell by the smirks on their faces that I looked worse.

Boris lifted his paw to his cheek. "Well, you've still got something right here."

Doris grinned. "I think you should try the water."

I couldn't win. There was no way out of it. I was gonna have to stick my face in the cold dog water. Slowly I made my way past the two big dogs. As I got closer, they moved aside. I was face-to-face with their water bowl. Just me and the clear cool liquid. I slowly lowered my nose to the bowl.

"That's it. Just a little bit lower," Boris encouraged.

Quickly I dunked my entire face into the water. My wet fur felt heavy.

"Now what?" I asked.

"Here, just rub up against my fur," Boris said as he sat down on the porch.

I began with the left side of my face, wiping it gently against Boris. Then I switched sides. Several times I walked back and forth, trying to get the thick makeup off my fur.

"You need to rub harder. You're getting rid of some, but there's still a lot left," Boris barked. "Rub until my brown fur turns the color of that creamy stuff you're wearing."

I rubbed harder and harder. Finally I could see the red color coming off me and onto his light brown coat. It was working. I kept rubbing and rubbing. When I was done, Boris's fur had three different colors of makeup on it: pink . . . red . . . and purple. Boris rolled in the grass for a while, until the color faded.

"I think you'll just have to live with the smell for a few days. Well, unless you want to dip your entire body in the water," Doris said.

I shot off toward the oak tree and zoomed up into the high branches.

"No, no, no, no! I can live with the stink. Just don't make me get the rest of my body wet!"

I flew back down the tree and made a couple of loops through the yard. Getting my face wet drove me crazy, and I had to get rid of the extra energy that had built up. After a few laps around the yard, I slid to a stop at Boris's feet.

"You know, I'm glad I helped you guys get away from the dog police. But I can't stand Kylie," I said as I rolled in the grass a few times. "I'm glad to be here, safe with my friends."

"Thanks for saving us," Boris said. "It takes a true friend to go through such humiliation to rescue her buddies."

"Yeah," Doris agreed. "We really do appreciate you helping us. If it wasn't for you, we would be in the dog pound. When we were puppies, Boris and I got out of the fence. We were going to explore, but we ended up getting lost. The dogcatchers scooped us up and took us to the pound."

Boris grimaced. "That was scary. There was a beagle in the same cage as us, and all he did was cry and howl about never being able to see his People again. Good thing Mandy and Todd came to get us."

Doris jumped in. "Fortunately, we didn't have to stay there very long. That beagle said he had spent the night there on the cold cement floor."

I glanced over at Morris. He was still sitting by the fence.

"Where was Morris?" I whispered.

"You mean while we were in doggy jail?" Boris asked.

I nodded. "Yeah, did he get out with you?"

Doris took a quick look to make sure the Scottie wasn't listening. "Morris hadn't come to live with us yet. We were a year old when Mandy and Todd brought him home. They found him on a country road. He was all alone. Just him, a small empty plate, and a bowl with a little bit of water in it."

Boris chimed in. "His previous People were not very good to him. That's why he gets so scared around people."

"What did they do to him?" I asked.

"Well . . ." Doris started. "When he was really little, his very first People tried to sell him, but they couldn't. So they took him to the pound. He stayed there for a couple of days. Then a Man People, a Woman People, and a Little Girl People came and picked him out. He was very excited to have new People to love with. His Little Girl People loved him. She even played tug-of-war with him. One day the three People left Morris at home alone. He got scared, so he started chewing on shoes and socks and whatever else he could find."

"Oh, no, did he get in trouble?" I asked.

Doris shook her head. "No, it was worse. When they got home, they took him for a ride. That's when he got dumped on the side of the road. He tells us it got dark there five times before Mandy and Todd found him. He was just a puppy, so you can imagine how scared he was."

"I didn't know about that," I said. "I guess that explains why he didn't get too close to Fern. It must have taken him a long time to trust Mandy and Todd."

Boris nodded. "Doris and I spent many hours convincing him that Mandy and Todd would love him no matter what and they would never leave him in a scary place."

I stared at the long shadows in the yard. "I guess I'd better start home," I said. "I'm getting pretty tired."

"Bye!" howled Boris and Doris in unison. I

took another glance at Morris. He was still chewing on his piece of rope and didn't even bother to look up.

I jumped over the fence and sneaked home. I knew Kylie didn't go too far from her own yard, but I wasn't going to take any chances. Plus, I didn't want Max to see me if he and his People were out. When I got to my house, I hid in the shadows of the bushes near the front window. I made my way around to the back door and waited for Carol to let me in. The sun disappeared. A chill filled the air. I curled up in a ball. *Maybe Morris will be in a better mood tomorrow. If he is, I can show them the meadow. We can have a lot of fun there*, I thought.

"Hon, would you go call Kikki, please? I'll get her supper ready," I heard Carol holler at Bill.

I jumped to my feet. I was starving. Bill opened the door.

"Kikki, it's suppertime!" Bill yelled without looking down. I slipped in the door, rubbing against his legs.

"There you are," he said. "You must be hungry. I didn't even have to holler twice."

Bill swooped me up in his arms and scratched my forehead.

"Whew." Bill's nose wrinkled. "What's that smell?"

He fanned his face and quickly put me down in the kitchen next to my food bowl. The tuna was irresistible. I gobbled it up. When I finished, I wobbled into the living room, where both my People were sitting in front of the TV. Well, Carol was reading a magazine, and Bill was flipping through channels with his remote control. I hopped onto Bill's lap and kneaded his tummy with my paws.

"Ouch!" he yelled as I tried to make myself comfy. "Just lie down, Kikki. What did you get into today?" Bill stretched his face as far away from me as he could. He cupped his hand over his nose.

I tucked my paws up under my body and fell asleep.

CHAPTER 5

"**G**ood morning, Kikki." Carol reached over and petted me.

Sitting on the bed next to me, Carol was putting on her makeup. I cringed because the powdery stuff reminded me of Kylie. Bill rushed around the house, trying to find his belt. *Today must be a workday*, I thought to myself. Carol worked at her father's flower shop. That was where I first met her.

When I was a baby, my first People took me and my brothers and sisters to the flower shop. They put bows on us and carried us in a big basket. When Carol peeked inside, I stretched up and licked her on the nose. She gave a little giggle and grabbed me up into her arms before I could blink.

"I want this one," she said. A huge grin made her face look even prettier.

Bill was surprised when Carol brought me home. But when I licked him, too, he decided they would keep me. That's how I came to live with Bill and Carol.

"Carol, where did you put my brown belt?" Bill asked, startling me out of my memory.

She gave a little snort, got up off the bed, and walked into the closet. "It's right here, where it belongs."

I stood up on the bed and stretched. On workdays Bill usually let me outside early if the weather was nice. I watched as Bill put his belt on and then gave Carol a kiss.

"Don't forget to put Kikki out," she called.

Bill grabbed me up and carried me outside. He plopped me down on the porch and got in his truck. As soon as his taillights disappeared around the corner, I bolted across the street. I had decided that Morris would be in a better mood, so I was going to take them to the meadow. I hopped over the gate and ran up to Morris's doghouse. Remembering what the big dogs told me, I figured if I suggested to Morris that we go to the meadow, maybe he wouldn't get mad.

"Wake up, sleepyhead!" I shouted.

Morris sprang to his feet. "Kikki? What are you doing?"

I gave him a quick kiss on the cheek with my rough tongue. "Get up, I'm going to take you to the meadow today. Let's go. Did you have your breakfast?"

Morris wagged his tail. "We always have a little nap right after breakfast. I'll wake Doris and Boris."

He ran to the big dogs' houses and barked until they got up. Then all three dogs ran to the fence, and got in their places to open the gate. Their tails wagged back and forth at the same time, like windshield wipers chasing away the rain.

"Okay, I'm coming." I laughed.

I hopped onto the fence post near the latch. "One, two, three."

As I said three, Morris hit the latch with his nose. I stuck my paw out to grab it. When I had a good hold of it, Morris pulled the gate toward him while Boris got his nose between the fence post and the gate.

"Hey, we're getting pretty good at this, aren't we?" Doris chuckled.

"Let's run," I said.

I took off toward the meadow with the three dogs trotting close behind. I dodged in and out of parked cars and leaped over bushes near the sidewalk. I slowed down when I got to the corner. I didn't want my friends to get lost.

"This way," I meowed. "It's right over there."

The three dogs paused. "Wow, that's really pretty. It's bigger than I thought it would be. And the pond, it's big, too." Doris couldn't hide her amazement.

"First, I need to warn you. See where that big red tractor is? Don't go near it. There's a big stinky hole out there that used to be part of an outhouse."

"A what?" Boris interrupted.

"An outhouse," I explained. "It's like an old-time port-a-potty. The actual outhouse was blown over by a storm, but the hole is still there. It's really deep and smells bad. If you fall in, you can't get out, so be careful."

I slipped under the barbed-wire fence. "Watch the thorny things. They really hurt if they grab you."

Boris found a loose spot in the fence that was big enough for his round body to squeeze through without scraping the barbs. Doris followed him, but Morris tried to get through the same spot I did. He let out a small whimper as one of the metal prongs scratched his back. I rolled my eyes.

Good grief! I told him to be careful. He's just got to do things his own way I guess.

"Can we get a drink from the pond? I'm really thirsty," Boris panted.

Doris was panting, too.

"Sure, just be careful of the cows. They're really big. I don't get close to them because I nearly got stepped on the last time."

Morris trotted off in front of us. Boris and Doris poked along behind, their noses whiffing every inch of ground they passed. I followed several steps behind Morris. I was glad he was acting better. A high-pitched yelping sound stopped me in my tracks. When I looked back, the big dogs were gone. Then, out of the corner of my eye, I saw Boris bouncing his way across the field. Doris was running a zigzag pattern behind him.

"There she goes," I heard Boris yelp.

Doris barked back. "Yeah, I see her. She's in the rotted-out tree trunk over there to your right."

Morris followed them through the tall weeds, his tail sticking up straight like a flagpole. It was all I could see peeking above the tall dried grass. The three of them stood near the old tree trunk, their noses whiffing the ground below as their tails waved high in the air. I had to see what the fuss was all about. I sped across the meadow to investigate.

"Hey guys, what is it?" I shouted.

Doris looked down at me. "We're not real sure. We've never seen one of these before."

"Well, scoot back a little so I can see, too," I said as I pushed my way past Morris.

It was dark inside the hollow tree trunk. I

tried to sniff and tell what it was, but all I could smell was Morris's dog breath. I heard a few squeaks coming from the tree. Cautiously I crawled a little way into the trunk.

I chuckled. "It's a bunny, you guys."

"A what?" Boris's ears perked up. "What in the world is that?"

I rolled my eyes. "Don't tell me you've never seen a bunny rabbit. I know you've never been to the meadow before, but surely you've seen a bunny."

"Nope, never seen one. Never even heard of one. It walked funny. I guess it didn't really walk, it kinda leaped or hopped like a frog." Doris chuckled.

Morris backed away from the tree and sat down. His eyes were fixed on the dead stump where the little rabbit was hiding.

"Hey," he whispered. "Maybe if we're really quiet, she'll come out. She might want to play, but she's just scared."

The four of us sat together . . . silent . . . still . . . waiting. We waited and waited and waited. Finally I saw a white streak out of the corner of my eye.

"There she goes. Let's follow."

By the time I finally got to my feet, the three dogs were down by the pond. They were chasing the poor bunny across the dam. She was at least ten feet in front of them and gaining more and more distance with each hop. I guess they didn't care because they just kept running. I wandered to the pond. I could see that the dogs had stopped in the distance. Their sides rapidly moved in and out and their tongues nearly dragged the ground.

"Did you give up?" I hollered.

"Yeah, she disappeared in the tall grass. I don't think she wants to play today. She just needs some time to get used to us," Doris wolfed.

They were headed back to the dam, so I strolled down to the water's edge to get a quick drink. The water wasn't very clear, but it was cool and refreshing.

SPLASH!

I jumped back from the edge as soon as a drop of water hit me. In the pond I could see a large rippling wave. Morris and Doris were standing on land directly across from me. Boris was nowhere in sight.

"Where did Boris go?" I asked.

Doris rolled her eyes. "Oh, he thought he saw a fish, so he dived in after it."

"Well, aren't you going to save him? He's so big, he'll probably drown!" I screamed.

"Don't worry. He's a good swimmer," Morris said.

I looked back at the water. Several bubbles floated to the surface. I could see Boris's big brown nose headed up for air.

"See, I told you."

Boris held a large trout in his mouth. He flinched as the fish's tail slapped him on the cheek.

"Wook wha I foum!" Boris mumbled.

"What did you say?"

He dropped the fish into the water. "I said, look what I found. Oops, where did it go?"

His eyes darted back and forth as he watched the fish disappear beneath the shimmering surface. His ears perked and he pounced. Once again he vanished into the pond. Doris sat next to me as we watched to see what Boris would have in his mouth this time. When Boris came up for air, his mouth was empty.

His eyes were wide. "You should have seen the fish I caught underwater. It was huge."

"Well, what did you do with it?" Doris asked.

"I, uh, I had to let it go. It finned my mouth. I must say it didn't feel good."

I watched as Boris dragged himself out of the pond. When he shook, sprays of water filled the air.

"We'd better head back home," Doris said, shaking some of the droplets from her coat. "I don't want to get in trouble for being out of the yard."

"Yeah, Doris is right," Boris agreed. "We don't want Mandy and Todd mad at us."

Morris wandered off in the opposite direction. "I'm not through exploring. You can go home, but I've got better things to do."

"There may be scary things out," Doris barked.

Morris just ignored the three of us and continued to sniff the ground, getting farther and farther away.

Boris shrugged his enormous ears and headed for home. Doris and I followed. Doris turned back to see where Morris was going.

"I forgot that Kikki was supposed to suggest things to Morris. I should have kept my mouth shut."

Boris shook his head. "Don't worry about it, Doris. We'll just go on home and see if he follows."

The three of us headed on toward the fence.

"Remember to be careful with those thorny things on the wire," I reminded them as I crawled under.

"Where did Morris go? He didn't even try to follow us, did he?" Boris said as he looked back toward the pond.

Boris stretched his neck.

"Do you see him?" Doris asked.

Boris nodded, then looked at me. "Didn't you tell us not to go over by the old red tractor, Kikki?"

"Yeah! Why?"

Boris shook his head in shame. "That's right where he's headed."

The three of us took off running toward the tractor.

"Keep your eyes on him," I told Boris.

Boris led the pack. Doris was right behind him and I took up the back position. We were running full speed ahead. Then, without warning, Boris stopped in his tracks. Since Doris was following too close, her face smacked into his rump.

"What's the matter, Boris?" I asked.

"He's gone. He just disappeared. I could see his ears above the grass and part of his face, then all of sudden—he just disappeared."

CHAPTER 6

My legs trembled as we ran toward the spot where we last saw Morris. I was so scared. If he really fell in the hole, he wouldn't be able to get out! The hole was so deep I'd only seen the bottom a few times when the sun was straight overhead. The big dogs were getting farther ahead of me.

"Wait!" I yelled.

They slowed down.

"Let me run ahead of you. I know where the hole is. I don't want you two to fall in with Morris. There's no way I could get all three of you out of there. Plus, I'm smaller. The dirt around the hole is a little loose, and if you get

71

too close, it might collapse."

"You're right, Kikki. Run ahead and we'll stay back a ways," Doris said.

Why couldn't Morris have listened to me? My heart raced as I got closer and still couldn't see him. Boris and Doris trotted up behind me.

Eyes wide, I stopped at the edge of the hole. "I can't see him."

I glanced back over my shoulder to make sure the big dogs didn't bump into me and accidentally push me in. They stopped a few feet behind.

"He must have fallen in," I meowed back to the other two dogs.

I crouched down next to the giant black hole. "Hello down there. Morris, can you hear me?"

The only voice that came to me from the depths of the hole was my own. No sounds from Morris . . . not a whimper, not a whine, not a cry. Nothing. The corners of my eyes filled with tears.

I couldn't look at Boris or Doris. "He's gone," I sniffed.

The three of us cuddled next to one another.

As we sat together, a tiny snickering noise came from behind one of the huge black tires of the tractor. My eyes flashed. Then my face burned with anger.

"Morris," I hissed. "That better not be you back there. I'm going to be so mad at you for not answering when I called your name."

I saw his sharp, white ears poke out from behind the tire.

"You make me so mad," Boris growled at Morris. We thought you were dead, and you think it's funny!"

I glared at Morris. "I don't know what your problem is, but you'd better straighten up. We're going home whether you like it or not."

Doris didn't need to say a word. Always sweet and tender, her unnatural look told Morris that we were all mad at him.

We turned our backs on Morris and started for home again. He followed, quite a ways behind us. It was a slow quiet walk. No one talked and no one looked back. When we reached the barbed-wire fence, the three of us went through, one at a time. We still didn't turn to see what Morris was doing. We just kept walking. When we rounded the corner near the house, Doris stopped and faced us.

When she did, her ears drooped. "He's not behind us."

Boris pushed the gate open with his head. "That's okay, just leave the gate and he'll get here on his own. Hopefully he's taking the time to think about how badly he scared us. I sure don't know what's gotten into that dog, but I hope he pulls out of it. He just isn't himself lately and he's causing us a lot of grief."

Doris's sweet face drooped to a frown. "And to think I tried to defend the way he was acting yesterday."

"Yeah, why did you do that? It's not good to defend that kind of behavior," Boris growled.

Doris glared at him. I stood back. The three of us went our separate ways. Doris went to her doghouse. Boris went to the porch. I sat down by the shed. The day sure had turned out to be a bad one. I wanted to talk to Charlie, but he was inside the People house. So, I curled into a ball and waited for Morris to return. Finally he pushed through the gate. He didn't look at us. He just walked in, sat down by the fence, and started chewing on an old wiggy.

"I'm exhausted." I yawned. "I'd better get to my house."

Doris helped me close the gate. "See you later."

I tried to smile. "Bye."

I crossed the street and stood in my yard, looking back at my friends' gate. It had been a perfectly good day. We chased a bunny, caught fish, and romped in the meadow. It was fun until Morris messed it up. I was mad at him for disobeying my warning, I was mad at him for being mean and insensitive. I was mad at him for being so stubborn. He played a joke and overdid it. With a sigh, I headed for the house. Maybe things would be better tomorrow.

After two weeks things still weren't much better. I went to see the dogs a few times. One day we even decided to go see Fern. On the way we saw Kylie prowling near her house. We could tell she was on the hunt for a cute little kitty or a puppy. She peered in our direction. We didn't want her to catch us, so we ran back home. A few days later Morris came up with the idea that we could go down the alley to get to Fern's. That way we could avoid Kylie. We tried it. Fern was happy to see us. She even fed us a little leftover hamburger meat. Morris still wouldn't get close to her, though. We took the alley again on the way home, but we ran into Kylie. She held a squirming kitty in her arms. We watched as she tried to stuff the poor thing in her pink backpack. It was a cat I had never seen before. The poor creature kicked and hissed, trying to get away. We ran all the way home as fast as we could. We didn't leave the yard after that. We were stuck . . . afraid Kylie would capture us and afraid of the dog-catchers. No one wanted to play games because we were afraid someone would get mad. Two weeks of doing nothing was pretty boring. I was going nuts.

I jumped up on the ledge where Charlie was taking a catnap.

"Charlie, I'm bored. Things just aren't fun," I meowed.

Charlie lifted an eyebrow. "You're bored?"

"Yeah." I nodded. "We don't do anything

anymore. We just sit around and sleep all day."

Charlie's whiskers twitched. He tilted his head to one side. "When was the last time you and the dogs had a good time?"

I hesitated. "Well . . . I guess it was when we went to the meadow. It's nice to go visit Fern, but everywhere we go, we see Kylie. I'm terrified that she'll catch me again."

"Well," Charlie purred. "Maybe you should suggest going back to the meadow. I've never been there. Maybe I'll go, too. Kylie doesn't go there, does she?"

My eyes flashed. "No, she doesn't . . . at least I've never seen her there." I felt my whiskers spring up. "I'll see if the dogs want to go."

I trotted over to the middle of the yard. "Charlie and I are going to the meadow. Does anyone want to go with us?"

Morris's ears perked up and his tail waved back and forth, but he didn't answer. Boris and Doris looked at each other, not knowing what to say.

Tail still wagging, Morris ran to the fence.

I winked at Charlie. "I guess Morris wants to go."

Charlie purred. "What about you two?

Would you like to go with us?"

"It should be okay, don't you think?" Boris whispered to Doris.

Doris wagged her tail and charged toward the fence. "Count us in!"

Boris galloped behind her.

"Thanks, Charlie," I said. "That was a good idea. Are you ready?"

Charlie stretched. "I'm ready. I feel pretty good today, but if I lag behind a little, don't worry."

We took our places at the fence.

"Ready? Now," I commanded.

We opened the gate and shot off for the meadow. I watched as the three dogs ran ahead of me. They were playing chase. I looked back at Charlie. He wasn't too far behind.

This is going to be a good day, I thought to myself.

CHAPTER 7

Thoughtful for once, Morris found a place big enough for Boris to fit through and eased carefully under the barbed-wire fence. The big dogs followed.

"Charlie," I said. "I'm glad you decided to come with us."

Charlie nodded, then slipped under the fence. "Well, I think we'll have a good time. It's nice to get away from the house every once in a while. I needed to stretch my legs a little."

The three dogs galloped toward the pond. They were still romping and playing. Morris bumped Boris, who gave him a playful growl, then both of them raced up on either side of

Doris. They squeezed together and pinned her, for a moment, between them. Her tail wagged back and forth. When they got to the edge of the pond, Boris jumped in.

"Watch this," I said to Charlie. "He can catch fish."

Charlie stopped a few feet short of the water. "Yes, I've seen him do that once or twice, back where we used to live. The first time he did it, I was afraid he would drown. I'd never seen a dog dive under water before."

I plopped down in the cool dirt next to Charlie. Morris and Doris laughed as Boris brought a huge fish up out of the water. The gray thing flipped and flopped in his mouth as he struggled to hold on to it. He swam to the shore with it still in his mouth. Its tail kept whacking him on the head. Boris struggled to pull his large body out of the pond. He dropped the fish on the dirt in front of the other two dogs.

Morris whiffed at it. The thing slapped him in the nose with its tail. Ears perked, Morris yanked his head back. "Wow! That's a big fish. I've never seen anything like it. How did you catch it?"

Boris stood tall and puffed out his chest. "It was a piece of cake. Nothing to it at all."

Doris rolled her eyes.

"You just dive down and pull one up. The big ones are slow. They don't have a chance with me in the water!" Boris bragged.

While the dogs were talking, Charlie and I watched the fish wiggle itself back to the water and swim away. Charlie chuckled.

"I guess that one got away." I giggled.

Doris left the other two dogs and headed toward us. She continued to roll her eyes as Boris talked.

Doris pointed her nose past the old red tractor. "Kikki, what's that over there?"

Charlie and I turned to see what she was looking at.

"I think it used to be a milk barn, when people lived here. Would you like to check it out? I've never really been up close to it. If we go, we'll have to walk way around the tractor. You don't think Morris will try to scare us again, do you?"

Doris looked at the two dogs by the pond. "No, I think he's learned his lesson."

Charlie and I stretched as we lifted ourselves off the ground. Charlie licked some of the dust from his sides. Boris and Morris were talking about the fish, still not realizing it had wiggled itself back into the water. I walked up to the two of them.

"See that old building over there?"

They stretched their necks to see it.

"No, that way," I said, pointing with my nose.

Boris's eyes got big. "The one past the tractor?"

"Yeah," I said. "Do you want to go explore? I've never been in there before, and I thought it might be fun to see what is in it."

The two dogs looked at each other and wagged their tails.

"Let's go," Morris woofed as he took off for the old barn.

"Wait," I hissed. "That deep hole really scares me."

I looked Morris straight in the eye. "Let's go way around to the side. Okay?"

For an instant Morris's pointed ears flattened against his head, then they perked up.

"Okay." He smiled.

Boris and Doris ran after him. I stayed back far enough that I could keep an eye on the dogs and watch out for Charlie, who was bringing up the rear. Morris made a wide arc around the tractor and the hole. Once I was certain the dogs were past the danger area, I glanced back to see how Charlie was doing. I knew he was old and his legs might be hurting him. To my surprise, he was stretched up on his hind legs, swatting at something with his front paws. Old Charlie was acting like a kitten! I giggled as the yellow butterfly he was chasing flew out of his reach. It would dance in front of him for a minute, but when Charlie stretched for it, the butterfly darted away. He was feeling pretty young, I guess, since he was playing so much. I turned to check on the dogs. All three of them had their noses buried in the ground around the barn. Boris pushed Doris out of his way, trying to beat her to all the new smells. I ran to catch up with them, leaving Charlie behind.

"Did you find anything interesting?" I asked Doris.

"No. There are a lot of new smells that I don't recognize, though."

Boris and Morris worked their way around the side of the barn. Every once in a while, Morris stuck his nose down deep in the dirt. His tail waved high in the air as he sniffed.

"Let's go see what's inside," I suggested.

Doris nodded her head, and we found a hole between some rotted boards, the other two dogs followed. Except for a few old empty crates, the barn was bare. Some leaves and several pieces of trash scampered about in front of the wind. Morris walked up and down the length of the barn, not missing an inch of ground.

"I've got a good whiffer," he bragged. "I smell a familiar scent, but I'm not sure what it is. It's not a good smell."

Suddenly Boris stood tall. He tilted his head first to one side, then the other.

"Shhhhh. I hear something," he whispered.

He ran over to where some boards were missing. With his paws on either side of the opening, he jumped up so he could see out. Suddenly his whole body froze.

"Oh, my gosh!"

"What's wrong? Is it Charlie?" I asked.

Boris shook his head. "Not yet, but we better get him out of here before she sees him."

He didn't have to say any more. *She* could only mean one person. . . . Kylie had invaded the only safe place we had to play. We had to get Charlie and ourselves out of here.

I jumped onto Boris's back and crawled up to his shoulders, so I could see out, too. Kylie had squeezed herself through the barbed-wire fence. Her body made it, but part of her dress stuck to one of the barbs.

"We've got to get out of here!" I yelled. "We better go now while she's trying to get her dress off the fence."

"Run!" Boris screamed. "Oh, there's Charlie, I'll warn him, you guys just run. We'll meet at the house."

Morris looked up for a second, then went right back to smelling the floor. Outside again, we could see Boris sneaking over to Charlie, his body low to the ground. He whispered something to the old cat, then Charlie turned to see Kylie. She was bopping across the field, getting closer and closer. She watched the ground in front of her, and every once in a while she would reach down and pick up a weed. We could see Charlie's body tense. He leaped on to Boris's back and Boris took off. They caught up with us and we all scurried through the fence. We turned back to make sure Kylie hadn't seen us. She was wandering closer and closer to the barn.

"Whew, we made it. She didn't even see us," Boris panted.

I took a deep breath and slowly blew out the air. "I guess we're not safe anywhere we try to go. We just can't get away from her."

Charlie was panting, too.

"So, that's Kylie. She doesn't seem that bad," he teased.

I shook my head. "Well, you haven't seen her close up. And I guarantee you don't want to."

We walked at a brisk pace back to the house. Charlie and I hurried through the gate first. Boris and Doris followed us, then shut the gate behind them.

"We can't get away from Kylie," Boris groaned.

I looked around the yard. Morris wasn't there. We were in such a hurry to get away from Kylie, we forgot to make sure we were all together.

"Hey, guys, where's Morris? I thought he would follow us," I said.

Doris frowned. "Yeah, I did, too. I guess the last time I saw him, he was still smelling the floor of the barn. I just thought Morris would be right behind us."

"Don't worry, I'm sure he's fine. He's probably just hiding from Kylie. He'll be home shortly," Boris assured us.

Charlie groaned. "I'm worn out. I'm going to take a nap. If Morris doesn't come home soon, you might want to go look for him. You need to stay together, though. Kylie's more likely to leave you alone if you're in a group."

Charlie curled up on the mat near the back door. I followed the fence line with my eyes to make sure Morris wasn't hiding anywhere. I even checked the spots where his wiggy pieces were piled up.

My stomach turned flip-flops. "I hope she didn't get him. I would feel so terrible."

"Well, Kikki," Boris said. "It might not be such a bad thing if she did catch Morris."

I frowned at him. "What do you mean? Kylie would dress him up and put makeup on his face. She'd probably put perfume on him, too. Let me tell you, that's *NOT* a good thing."

Doris shook her head. "I think he just means that Morris would learn a lesson from it."

Boris nodded his head in agreement. "That's right. He might learn to respect us more and listen to what we say. We don't say things to be bossy. Usually, we have a pretty good reason for telling him stuff."

I let out a big sigh, then walked over to one of Morris's wiggy pieces and curled myself into a tight ball. The big dogs sat down next to the gate, waiting on Morris. I didn't agree with them. Even though Morris had been snotty lately, I didn't want him to have to endure the humiliation. No one should have to experience . . . Kylie.

CHAPTER 8

"Help, let me in! Hurry!"

The loud yapping startled me. I sprang to my feet. My tail fuzzed. Boris and Doris rushed to the gate growling, and Charlie leaped to his feet, his back arched.

"Come on, guys. It's me, Morris. Let me in."

Boris and Doris frowned. I could hear them mumbling to each other.

"Should we let him in or just leave him out there?" Boris whispered.

"Leave him until he gets that attitude adjustment he's been needing," Doris mumbled.

The two big dogs arched their ears toward the gate to see what Morris would say.

"Guys, this isn't funny. Please let me in."

Boris began to whiff the air. Then he chuckled. He turned to me and mouthed, "She caught him all right. Smells like perfume."

My stomach turned at the thought.

"Is that a pretty girl behind this gate?" Boris teased.

I ran over to the big dogs and jumped up on the post. I looked down. "We've got to let him in, you two. He's really scared."

Morris's legs trembled underneath the bright yellow dress he was wearing.

Boris frowned. "Serves him right."

"I agree, but I wouldn't wish that type of punishment on anyone. Not even my worst enemy. Not even Max."

The looks on the big dogs faces turned from joking to serious. They knew I wasn't playing around.

I looked Doris in the eye. "On the count of three, you have to jump up and hit the latch with your nose. Morris can't do it from the other side. Can you handle it?"

Her expression was serious. "I'll do my best."

"Boris, do what you usually do."

He nodded his head. They both knew I meant business. When Boris pulled the gate open with his shoulder, Morris shot through.

"Hurry, close it!" he said as he pushed on it. The big dogs helped him shut the gate.

Morris hesitated, his eyes focused on the ground. "I'm sorry I teased you, Kikki, after Kylie caught you. I didn't realize how horrible it was. At least not until now."

The two big dogs were standing tall behind me. Morris looked at both of them.

"Boris . . . Doris . . . I'm sorry I didn't listen to you when you told me to run. From now on I'm going to do anything you tell me to do."

I looked over my shoulder at the two big dogs. They were grinning at each other.

"Anything?" Boris chuckled.

Morris thought for a second. "Almost anything!"

"Okay, let's get him out of that dress," I said. "I know how uncomfortable it is. The lace is itchy, and it's hard not to step on it when you walk."

Morris sat down so we could figure out what to do. A yellow ribbon was tied in a bow, holding the dress together. I pulled on one of the loops with my paws. When it didn't give, I pulled harder. I even tugged on it with my teeth. Finally the loop pulled loose and I began working on the other one. When it came loose, I was left with a knot.

"Move aside," Boris said. "I'll just gnaw it with my teeth. I guess it's a shame Morris can't reach it. The way he chews on rope, he'd have that dress off in no time."

Doris chuckled. "That's the truth!"

Boris tugged and chewed and gnawed and pulled. Snarling at the knot, he even lifted Morris clear off the ground. Finally the ribbon broke and Morris dropped out of the dress, plopping on the ground. I had to admit that he looked pretty funny with all the makeup on his face. When we got the dress off him, Morris tried to rub the makeup on the dry grass. It was quite a sight. His rump was high in the air, while he pushed his face across the ground, one side, then the other. Then he flopped over on his back. His short white feet waved in the air. Morris squirmed and wiggled. Twisting side to side, he nearly touched his tail with his nose.

Boris stood back, watching, trying not to laugh. "Did you get the stink off?"

"No, not yet, still working on it," Morris said as he continued to wiggle on his back.

I looked over toward the dogs' water bowl. "You could try sticking your head in the water."

Morris's eyes got wide and he stopped moving. "Uh, no," he said abruptly.

I guess he didn't like to get his face wet, either. Morris went right back to wiggling again. He tried for so long to get the smell and the makeup off that he finally wore himself out. I felt sorry for Morris. I just wanted to go home and sit in Bill's or Carol's lap. To feel safe and warm and . . .

"Kikki? You okay?" Doris asked.

"Yeah, I'm just tired. It's been a long day."

Doris shook her head. "Yes, it has. You'd better go home and get some rest."

I said my good-byes and hopped over the gate. I slinked carefully across the yard, checking all around me for Kylie. When I felt the coast was clear, I sped across the street, around the house, and in through the back door, safe and sound.

CHAPTER 9

TRAPPED!

That's all there was to it. All of us were . . . trapped!

There was no pen, no cage, no fence, but all of us—Charlie, me, the three dogs—Boris, Doris, and Morris—the whole pack of puppies—we were all . . . trapped! It was like Kylie—without even being there—had built an invisible barrier around us. I never ventured farther than my own yard or the puppy pack's yard. While all the other kids in the neighborhood were at school, Kylie was always home and we never knew when she would be outside. We decided maybe her mom taught her school at home. I've seen them sitting on the porch with really big books and lots of paper. Plus, I had to keep an eye out for Max when I was not with my friends.

Morris was even worse. We couldn't get him to go anywhere. He was definitely a different dog after his run-in with Kylie. He was real quiet and never argued with Boris and Doris. In a way it was nice. In another way . . . well . . . it just wasn't Morris. He spent a lot of time alone, chewing on his wiggy or gnawing on little pieces of rope. He always let Boris and Doris eat first and wouldn't go near the gate.

A week or two of just sitting around the backyard got really old.

One afternoon Charlie and I tried to talk them into going to the meadow. When I left my house that day, I saw Kylie and her mother drive off in their car, so I knew it would be safe. Everyone was excited and ready to go, but when we got to the gate, Morris stopped.

"You guys go ahead." He sniffed, with a little wag of his tail. "I think I'll just stay here."

Charlie and I tried to convince him that it was okay.

"I saw her leave," I said. "She can't get us."

Morris wouldn't budge. He insisted that we go without him, so we headed for the meadow. We took a few steps and Doris—always the motherly one—stopped and turned back.

"Go on and play. I don't want Morris to feel lonely."

The rest of us didn't even get across the street when Charlie stopped. "I'd better stay with them. My legs are a little stiff today."

We never made it to the meadow.

Three weeks of just sitting around the backyard was driving all of us crazy. It was so boring that even Boris and Doris got cross with each other. For no reason, Boris lost his temper and snapped at her. That was *not* like Boris at all. He was the biggest, scariest-looking dog in the world, but he was a gentle giant. No matter what happened, he always kept his cool. He never even growled at anyone.

Something had to give.

On Saturday morning Carol didn't let me run out the door like she usually did. She picked me up and walked out to the flower garden in the front yard. She put me down beside her and started digging in the soft dirt to plant tulip bulbs. Bill came out and sat on the front porch to drink his coffee.

It was a pretty day—bright and warm. For a while I played with the wiggle worms that peeked out of the freshly turned dirt. Then I stretched out to rub and scratch on the grass. A movement caught my eye. Charlie strolled across the front porch of his People's house. In one quick movement I leaped to my feet and darted across the street.

"Good morning, Charlie," I meowed. "What are you doing out in the front?"

"It's such a nice day to be outside. I was trying to sleep on the back porch, but the dogs kept bickering and fussing, so I figured I could stretch out in the sunshine here."

I always wanted my friends to meet Bill and Carol.

"Charlie, I've got an idea," I said. "Let's get the dogs and I'll introduce you to Bill and Carol, my People. Kylie won't bother us with my People outside, and maybe it'll keep the dogs from fighting for a few minutes."

Charlie nodded. "Sounds like a plan to me. Go get them and I'll head on over to your house."

I made sure Charlie got across the street okay, then hopped up on the fence post.

"Okay, friends, it's time to break out of this place. We've been cooped up too long, so get over here and help me open this gate," I meowed.

Boris and Doris jumped to their feet and sprinted to the gate. Boris leaped up in the air a couple of times. His tail wagged.

"Where are we going?" he barked.

I looked down at him. "My People are outside this morning, and I want you to meet them. They're really nice. I think you're going to like them a lot."

Following the fence line with my eyes, I spotted Morris. He was sitting next to the garden pond with his wiggy between his front feet. Ears perked, he watched us. Small pieces of rope surrounded Morris. I could tell he'd been working on that wiggy for several hours.

"You're going, too!" I hollered at him.

His tail wagged, but he didn't budge.

"It's okay," I encouraged. "My People are outside in the front yard. Carol's digging in the dirt and Bill's sitting on the front steps. We'll be safe with them. They're big People and Kylie's just a little People. Bill and Carol can protect us."

Morris stood up, but his ears were flat against his head. He eased closer.

"I don't know," he whined. "What if Kylie gets us before we get across the street."

"She's not going to get us," Doris barked. "Number one . . . we'll all be together. Number two . . . Kikki's People will hear the commotion and come save us. And, number three . . . well, just stop worrying and let's go."

Doris leaped, trying to hit the latch with her nose, but missed. She looked down at Morris.

"I'm not very good at this part. Will you open it for me?"

Morris sidled up next to her. "Yeah, I've gotten pretty good at this."

Doris backed away, then looked up at me and winked. I nodded back at her.

"One. Two. Three."

When I got to three, Morris leaped, hit the

latch with his nose, and the gate opened. The three dogs dashed to the front of the house. They waited for me at the curb. Squeezing himself between the big dogs, Morris and the rest of us crossed the street together.

Carol was still sitting, digging in the dirt. Boris thundered toward her. Eyes wide, she braced herself. Boris knocked her over in the dirt and licked her face.

Bill jumped to his feet. "Are you okay, Carol?"

She was laughing so hard she couldn't answer. Bill let out a sigh when he realized Carol wasn't hurt.

"Come here, big guy," Bill called.

Boris ran over to him. Bill reached down and rubbed behind his ears, giving Carol time to stand up. She dusted off her pants, then kneeled down next to Doris and Morris.

"Hi, sweeties."

Doris leaned up against her on one side. Morris's tail wagged as Carol talked, but he kept his distance. It made me feel good to see them all get along. I walked over and lay down next to Charlie in the dirt.

"So, what do you think?" I asked.

Charlie flopped over on his back. "Your People are really nice. The dogs aren't fighting and we got Morris out of the yard. You're a pretty smart cat, Kikki."

A warm feeling tingled in my stomach. It made me feel good to have Charlie say I was smart. I really liked him and looked up to him.

Charlie flipped over onto his side. He chuckled. I turned to see what he was giggling about. Carol stood with her hands on her hips and her legs shoulder width apart. She was watching Bill play with Doris. Boris stood facing her, but Carol wasn't looking. There was a gleam in the enormous dog's eye.

Charlie grinned. "Watch this!"

About that time Boris trotted toward Carol, then crawled under her.

"He's so big, it looks like you're riding a horse," Bill roared.

Carol leaned down to scratch between Boris's shoulders. He looked back at her with a silly grin. She rubbed behind his ears, too. Charlie and I watched as Boris's back right foot thumped the ground. The more Carol rubbed his ears, the faster his leg thumped.

Bill was now on the stairs, sitting on the top step with Morris and Doris beside him. Morris seemed to be warming up to Bill. Whenever he'd stop petting them, Morris would nudge him in the side with his cold wet nose. Bill squirmed a bit, then went back to loving the Scottie. Doris acted like she wanted some attention, too. She licked the side of Bill's head. Wet and sticky, all the hair on the right side clumped together and stood straight up. Carol glanced at them and laughed so hard she had to sit down.

Finally everyone was calm. Carol scooted back over to her garden. Occasionally, she reached over and scratched Charlie and me on the head. Bill raked leaves out from under the bushes while the dogs slept on the porch. I must have dozed off, too, because next thing I knew, Bill and Carol were nowhere in sight. Jumping up real quick, I turned to look down the street.

Charlie opened one eye. "What's wrong?"

"Oh, I guess Bill and Carol went inside. I was just making sure Kylie hadn't sneaked up on us."

The dogs were still sleeping on the porch.

"Do you want to meet Fern? I haven't seen her in a long time and really would like some turkey and milk," I meowed.

Charlie stretched. "No, thanks. I better get home. Why don't you take the dogs with you. You'll be safer that way."

I nodded at him, then went over to wake the dogs. Charlie strolled home.

"Hey, guys," I whispered.

They opened their eyes. Morris jumped up and cowered by the door.

"It's just me," I meowed. "Let's go see Fern. It's been a long time since we've been there. I'm sure she misses us."

Morris shook his head. "No, I need to go home. You can go on without me."

I arched my back, fuzzed my tail, and hopped sideways until I was right in Morris's face.

"I've had it with this scared stuff," I hissed. "I've had it with you being scared to leave the yard, and I've had it with me so terrified I'll hardly go out alone. We're held prisoner by a little-bittie girl People. We're afraid to even cross the street because she might show up and grab one of us."

I wrapped my tail around my bottom and sat so I could rub my cheek against Morris's face. "It's not right to be afraid all of the time. We can't let her do this to us."

Morris took a deep breath and stood tall. "You're right, let's go."

CHAPTER 10

Fern was happy to see us. She was sitting in her rocking chair, humming a song. When she noticed us coming, she leaped up and went inside. Just as we got there, she stepped out holding a sack of turkey scraps in one hand and a bowl of milk in the other.

"Here, Kikki. This is for you," she said as she put the milk down in front of me.

I shared my milk with the dogs.

"Come here, puppies, this is for you." She waved the turkey in the air.

Boris clamored over to the porch swing where Fern sat. When he hopped up to put his paws beside her, he almost flipped her out of the swing.

"No, no, stay down."

Boris stood in front of Fern with one paw up on the swing. Fern tossed a piece of turkey behind him, so he would get down. Doris waited patiently. Since Doris was so gentle, Fern handed a slice of turkey to her. Calmly Doris took it out of her hand.

Fern looked over at me and Morris. "Come here, little guy. You need a piece of this, too."

I watched as Morris's tail wagged, but he didn't move.

Nudging him with my nose, I whispered, "Remember what I said about not being scared. You need to get some turkey."

Morris sighed, then took slow steps over to Fern. His tail wagged, but not very much.

"Here you go," Fern said, holding the piece of turkey out for Morris.

Cautiously he reached up and grabbed the turkey from her hands. Morris jumped back when he heard a car drive by.

"It's not Kylie," I meowed. "Stop being so scared."

It was easy for me to tell him that, but my insides jumped a little, too, when the car sped by. I finished drinking the cold milk and leaped up on the swing with Fern. She tore some turkey into small pieces and put it on my blanket. It was the first time in a long time that I had her turkey. It tasted so good. When I finished it, I crawled in her lap.

"Where have you guys been?" Fern asked. "I sure have missed your company lately."

She held me on her lap with one hand and reached down to pick up a blanket.

"See, I'm almost done with my great-granddaughter's blanket. She will be born in a week or two. Maybe you can meet her when she's a little older. I will tell her all about you."

I purred as Fern talked. I didn't realize how much I'd missed her sweet voice. She always talked to us as if we were People like her. I remembered her telling Teebo and me about her great-granddaughter. The last time I saw her working on the light pink blanket, it was very tiny. Now it was big . . . big enough to cover Boris *and* Doris. Usually it didn't take Fern very long to finish a blanket. I guess this was a very special blanket. She even put some yellow yarn in with the pink to make it look like little flowers. The outside edge was trimmed with the pretty yellow yarn. Her face gleamed as she worked on the blanket. She sang a quiet lullaby. If the dogs and I had not been so restless, she might have sung us to sleep. But, it felt like we had been asleep for weeks and we needed to romp and play.

I watched Morris. He puffed his chest out and barked, "Let's go to the meadow."

The big dogs looked back and forth. Their foreheads wrinkled.

"*You* want to go to the meadow?" Doris asked.

"That's right, let's go. I can't be scared and live like I'm in doggy jail. We've got to get out and live, have a good time. What do you say?" he howled.

I reached down and bopped him on the head. "Good for you. Let's go."

Stretching up toward Fern's face, I gave her a kiss on the cheek.

"Bye," the dogs barked in unison. "See you soon."

Fern looked a bit sad. "You're leaving already? Well, don't stay away so long next time. You're always welcome at my house."

She stood at the edge of the porch waving good-bye to us. The wind blew the bottom edges of her skirt around, and a few hairs were blowing loose from the bun at the back of her head.

Maybe I'll come back tomorrow and spend a little more time with her. I missed her too much, and she looked lonely standing there on the porch.

I meowed good-bye to her, then chased after the dogs. They were waiting by the street for me. Morris stood tall, but he managed to squeeze in between the two big dogs.

Boris looked down at him. "I'm proud of you. This is going to be a wonderful day. The sun is shining and we're headed to the meadow. Can't get much better than this."

We all felt good, I guess. We ran and jumped and leaped. Kylie was still in our minds, but mostly we didn't think about her. When we got to the meadow, we stayed close together. Each of us checked to make sure she wasn't around.

"Let's go back to the barn. We didn't get to explore much last time," I meowed.

Morris stopped walking.

"Be brave," Boris barked.

Morris took a huge breath and held his head high. "You're right. She's not here, and as long as I listen and pay attention we'll be fine."

"That's right, Morris. You can do it," Doris encouraged.

Together, we hurried to the barn. Boris sniffed around the door.

"Wait here. I'll make sure she's not inside."

After a few minutes Boris popped his head out of one of the windows. "It's safe to come in. Looks like the only thing in here is a squirrel's home. There's a nest-looking thing in the rafters."

The dog's ears perked when he said squirrel. They liked to tease them as much as Teebo and I had. We raced to the door and joined Boris inside.

"Look," Morris yipped. "There's some kind of nest in here, too. There are twigs and pine cones. Do you think it's a squirrel's? I didn't notice it last time."

Doris peeked in the crate. "Smells like squirrel. I wonder where they are."

I watched as the two dogs sniffed around the outside of the crate. Suddenly, out of nowhere, something flew from the rafters and bonked Doris on the head. Her ears flopped as she shook it off.

"Hey, what was that?"

Boris looked up in the rafters. "Looks like we found your squirrels."

We looked up just in time to see the bigger one hurl another acorn toward us. I ducked out of the way.

"That's Momma Squirrel. She used to live in the tree in your backyard. Teebo chased her one time. He almost fell in Max's yard following her. I haven't seen her since then. I guess she decided to move."

The puppy pack barked at the two squirrels. Acorns flew in every direction. I decided to peek out the door to make sure nobody was around. Quickly I circled the barn. No one was there, so I rejoined my friends inside. It was noisy. The dogs barked and the squirrels chattered.

"Get out of our barn," Momma Squirrel yammered.

"Your barn? I don't see your name on it,"

Boris barked. "I think you can share with us for a little while."

"No, this is our home for the winter. We're storing our food here so we don't starve, so I suggest you leave now. We don't share with anyone."

Doris frowned up at them. "If you're storing food for the winter, then why are you throwing it at us. Don't you know it's not nice to play with your food?"

Morris chuckled. "Yeah, not nice to play with food."

Before he had time to duck, Momma Squirrel pegged him with an acorn.

"I said get out," she chittered.

"Come on, guys. Let's go. We can explore other places. I don't feel like getting hit in the head with any more acorns today," I meowed.

I flipped my tail and waltzed out of the door. Morris followed close behind.

"I'm with you, Kikki. It doesn't feel too good to be hit with acorns."

After a few minutes the two big dogs ran out of the door giggling. Their laughter was contagious, and before we knew it, Morris and I were chuckling, too. We didn't even know what was funny. Finally, when we settled down, I asked what happened.

"Well," Boris started. "We were following you, but Doris got hit in the side by a flying acorn. We stopped and looked back just in time to see Momma Squirrel fall from the rafters. She threw the acorn so hard that she knocked herself right off her perch. She wasn't hurt, but boy was she mad."

We were so busy talking that none of us noticed how close we were to the tractor.

Doris stopped and sniffed at the air. "What's that smell?" Her nose crinkled.

We stopped and whiffed the breeze. It was a terrible odor, sort of a mixture of smells. We crept closer to the hole.

Morris turned to me. "What is it?"

"Not sure."

"It smells gross," Boris barked.

My nose wrinkled. "It smells like something has stirred up the stuff in the hole."

I hesitated for a second. "But there's another odor, too. I've smelled it before, I just can't figure out where."

Morris's ears perked. "What's that noise?"

"I don't hear anything," Boris barked.

"Shhhhh, there it is again. Sounds like someone crying," Morris yipped.

As we eased closer to the pit, the smell got stronger . . . and . . . worse. Morris peered over the edge. His tail puffed and the hair on his back ruffled. I ran to see what it was. At first I couldn't figure it out, but when I moved, the light hit her face. Her bottom lip quivered, and her dirty, chubby cheeks were streaked with tears. My fur fuzzed. Her arms stretched upward toward us. Boris and Doris eased up next to me.

"Ahhhh!" Kylie screamed.

The four of us ran for our lives. As we ran, I pictured the chubby little face staring up at us and her muddy cheeks, wet with tears. I could see her grubby hands opening and closing as if begging us for help. I slowed down, then stopped. The rest of the group kept running. After a few seconds Morris realized I wasn't following. He stopped, turned around, and walked over to me.

He looked me straight in the eye and shook his head. "You're going back, aren't you?"

I didn't answer.

"Why?" Morris asked.

I still couldn't answer him. All I could see were the scared brown eyes looking out of the darkness and the pudgy little hands reaching up for help.

CHAPTER 11

Morris stepped within a few feet of the hole. "I can't believe we're doing this."

I shook my head. "Me, either."

The crying got louder. Morris and I peered over the edge of the pit. Kylie leaned up against the side of the hole, her hands covering her face. When she realized we were there, she reached up to us again. Kylie looked helpless and scared. Suddenly her eyes flashed wide, and she let out another of her ear-piercing screams. When we jumped back from the hole, we noticed the big dogs standing there.

"How are we going to save her?" I meowed.

"Boris and I can jump down there. I'll stand

on him and Kylie can crawl up our backs," Doris barked.

I thought for a second. "But she's scared of you two. She might freak if you get down there with her."

"Yeah," Boris agreed. "Then how would we get out of there?"

"We're just animals. We're going to need help from people," Morris yapped.

I made a hard sprint for the barbed-wire fence. "Come on, let's get Mandy and Todd to help."

The dogs caught up with me.

"I heard them say they were going to the store today. I doubt that they're home yet," Morris barked.

"We can go look," Doris hollered.

When we got to their house, no one was there. Charlie was standing on the front porch looking for us.

"What's going on?" he asked.

"Kylie fell down in the hole where the old outhouse used to be. We need to get a People to follow us so they can get her out. I guess Mandy and Todd aren't back yet," Boris barked.

"No, they're still at the store. Maybe you can get Kikki's people to help. You'd better hurry though, they're getting in their car," Charlie meowed.

By the time we looked, they were already backing out of the driveway. We ran to catch them, but it was too late. We chased them to the corner, but they never saw us.

Charlie waved for us to come back. "I guess you can try Kylie's mom and dad, since no one else is home."

I rolled my eyes. "Well, if that's our only choice . . . let's go."

All five of us rushed over to Kylie's house. Boris scratched at the screen door with his front paw. No one answered. He scratched again and again. Still, nobody came to the door. Morris bumped the door with his side, trying to get someone's attention, but that didn't work, either.

I took a deep breath. "We're going to have to do this ourselves. We need a ladder or something."

Doris looked around. "Where are we going to get a ladder? There's no ladder, no rope, nothing."

"Oh, wait. Morris and I know where we can get a rope," I meowed.

"I remember quite well." Morris shook his head. "We need that rope. The one that the bucket was tied to. It hung over the limb and had a red brick tied to the other end. Kylie put us in that bucket and used the rope to lower us to the ground, when she was tired of playing with us." We followed Morris to the big tree in the middle of the yard.

I looked up at the limb with the rope draped over it. "How do we get it down?"

"Step aside," Boris barked.

He grabbed the rope with his teeth and started pulling. Morris jumped in to help. As the two of them backed away from the tree with the rope in their mouths, the bucket rose higher and higher.

"Ah, oh, now what?" Doris asked.

The bucket was caught under the limb. Doris and I tried to join in. We yanked and tugged, but the bucket wasn't going over. Finally we gave up and let go of the rope. It flew back to the same place where we started, brick and all.

"I've got an idea!" I yelled.

With my nose I pointed to the rope just above the brick. "Morris, get busy."

The three dogs and Charlie frowned at me.

Doris's expression changed first. She nodded. "Good idea, Kikki."

Boris nodded, too. "I see what you're saying."

Morris didn't understand. He looked at the rope, then turned his head from one side to the other.

"What do you mean? I don't understand," he barked.

"Wiggy!" I yelled.

Morris nodded his head. "Oh, okay. I see what you mean."

Suddenly Morris froze. His pointy ears perked. "Wait, I hear something. It must be Kylie's mom. She's calling her name."

"Is she headed toward the meadow?" Charlie asked.

"No, her voice is coming from the opposite direction. She went that way." He said, pointing past Fern's house with his nose.

"Let's go get her," I meowed.

Charlie turned to Morris. "Since you're good with chewing rope, you should stay here. That way, if they can't get Kylie's mom to follow, we'll at least have the rope so we can do it ourselves."

Morris nodded his head, then started chewing just above the knot.

"I'll go get Kylie's mom," Doris barked. "The rest of you stay here and help Morris. I'll be right back."

We watched Doris round the corner at the end of the street. Morris chewed and chewed. Before we knew it, pieces of rope were all over the ground near the brick.

Morris stopped a second. "Stand back, it's about to fall."

We stepped away from where the bucket dangled. With a few more nibbles the rope slid loose and the bucket clattered to the ground. We looked up just in time to see Doris zoom around the corner. Tail tucked, she ran as fast as she could.

"What's wrong?" Charlie asked.

"We've got to hurry," Doris panted. "I barked and barked at Kylie's mom, trying to get her to follow me. All she did was scream. Then she ran to a lady's door and started pounding on it and yelling for help. The lady let her in. She's probably calling the dog pound. If they catch us, Kylie will never get out of the hole. They'll never find her."

Boris picked up the bucket end of the rope. Morris grabbed a spot in the middle and Doris got on the chewed end.

"Maybe you and Morris should switch places," Charlie said to Doris. "You're a little bit taller, and that might help keep the rope off the ground."

The two dogs rushed to trade places and we took off for the meadow. Charlie and I led the way. We stopped several times so the dogs could get a better grip on the rope. One time Boris and Doris ran on opposite sides of a tree, flipping each other on the ground. The rest of us chuckled, but when they got to their feet it was back to business. There was a little problem when we got to the barbed-wire fence. Boris went through the loose wires with the bucket, but the rope drooped and got stuck on one of the barbs. I popped it loose with my paw. Boris continued to pull the rope slowly through the fence. But before it got to Doris's section, it caught on another barb.

"Try to go a little slower," Charlie meowed to Boris.

He nodded, then backed away slowly with the rope. I tried to guide it with my paw so it wouldn't catch on the barbs. Morris went through the fence next. The rope caught a few more times, but we finally got Doris through with the end of it. By the time we reached the hole, Kylie was in tears. The light was just right. We could see the muddy streaks running down her chubby cheeks.

"You came back for me?" she asked between sobs.

A warm feeling settled in my tummy. I knew we made the right decision.

"Okay, drop the bucket down to her," I meowed.

"No, wait," Charlie urged. "If you just drop it down there, she'll grab on to it and pull the entire rope in on top of her. She's pretty scared."

Charlie's whiskers twitched as he thought.

"I'll stay here and watch Kylie. You all stretch the rope out as far as it will go."

Boris put the bucket down near the hole, and we stretched the rope out so it was straight. We ran back over to Charlie.

"Now what?" Boris asked.

"Well, since you're the biggest and strongest, you need to be the one to pull her up."

Boris stood near the rope.

Charlie nodded. "Go ahead and pick it up. Kikki, you need to come over here and push the bucket so it goes in the hole. When she gets it over the edge, Boris, you need to walk slowly toward it. But be prepared to stop when I tell you to, and brace yourselves because Kylie will grab on as soon as she can reach it."

I ran to the bucket and pushed and shoved. The more I nudged, the closer it got to the edge. Finally it fell in. I stepped over to join Charlie.

"Okay, you can move forward slowly," I meowed.

Charlie and I watched as the bucket got closer and closer to Kylie. Her arms stretched upward, trying to reach it.

"Go real slow. It's almost to her," Charlie meowed.

The bucket dangled close to her chubby fingers. She leaped and hopped, trying to get hold of it.

"Brace yourself!" I yelled. "She's reaching for it."

About that time Kylie latched on to the bucket.

Charlie turned to Boris. "Move forward a little more so she can get the rope part."

He inched toward the hole and stopped. With both hands Kylie clenched the rope above the bucket.

"She's got it!" Charlie yowled. "You can start pulling her out."

Boris struggled as he tugged back on the rope. Doris ran over to help him. I peered down at Kylie. Her legs flailed as she tried to make her way up the side of the deep smelly pit. Suddenly her hands slipped from the rope. She struggled to grab the sides of the bucket. Morris rushed to join the other two dogs. They stopped and frowned. Looking back at Kylie, I realized she managed to latch on to the bucket.

Charlie was concentrating on Kylie, so I turned back to the dogs.

"It's okay. She slipped a little, but she's still there. Just a few more tugs and she'll be out."

They were tired but continued to pull. Kylie slipped again.

"I'm coming!" I yowled.

I ran over to grab onto the rope. With my claws and my teeth, I tried to help pull. Even Charlie rushed to join us. With all our strength, we made one more big tug. I looked back at Kylie. Her grubby fingers clawed at the grass around the edge of the hole. She fought to hold on but slipped again.

With his mouth full of rope, Boris mumbled, "We can't geh her ouh. Wha are we goin' do?"

Charlie let go of the rope. "I don't know, but we better do it quick. The pound truck just pulled up, over by the pond. I think he's seen us."

"If you all hol' on, I can 'rab the 'ack of her dress wif my teef and pull her ouh," Boris mumbled.

The four of us held on tight, while Boris let go. As soon as he did, we all slid toward the hole. Charlie almost fell in before Boris grabbed the rope again and pulled us back a little. We put so much energy into pulling that we were tired. Charlie released his hold for just a second.

"Don't give up," he encouraged. "You can't let go. We've got to keep trying."

All five of us pulled again. Exhausted, we started to slide back toward the hole. Our feet were braced, but it didn't help. I closed my eyes. We were going to fall in. When I blinked, I saw a hand reaching down for Kylie. It was the pound man. He grabbed the back of her dress and pulled. Boris, Doris, Morris, Charlie, and I fell backward and sat down on the ground with a thud. The black gunky stuff that Kylie had been stuck in plopped from her churning legs as the pound man lifted her away from the pit.

For just a second the man started to hug and comfort the crying child. Then the smell must have hit. He held her by the shoulders with his arms straight and his head leaned far to one side. His nose crinkled up.

"It's okay, you're safe now," the man gasped, patting her on the head.

Kylie dug the dirty crud from her eyes. The pound man wrinkled his nose and fanned his face. Then . . . Kylie spotted the dogs.

"Ahhhhh!" she screamed. In a flash she crawled up the pound man.

There was another scream. Kylie's mom rushed toward us.

"Oh, my! What have these horrible beasts done to my baby?" she squealed, snatching Kylie out of the man's arms. "Just look at that dress. It's dirty . . . and . . . whew . . . the smell!

The pound man shook his head. "Ma'am, these five animals tried to *save* your daughter's life. They were working to get her out of the hole when I got here. I've never seen anything like it before. They all worked together, struggling to rescue your daughter. These are some amazing animals."

He rolled his eyes when he realized that Kylie's mom wasn't listening to a word he said. Kylie just kept screaming. Kylie's mom put her down, and the two of them stormed off across the meadow.

The pound man reached down and petted each of us. "You did a really good job helping that little girl. Now, get back to your yard where you belong."

He strolled back to his truck and gave us a big smile and wave. The five of us headed back to the Puppy Pack's yard.

Once safe behind the closed gate, I turned to the dogs.

"Did we do the right thing?"

"I don't know." Morris shrugged. "Kylie is still Kylie."

"Yeah, and we even let the dogcatcher get close enough to catch us. All for her," Boris barked.

I looked at Charlie. "What do you think?"

He turned to me with a knowing look. "Well, how do you feel about it?"

"I think Kylie will always be Kylie."

"No." Charlie grinned. "How do you *feel* about it?"

"I guess I feel dumb. Kylie is always going to try to catch me and Morris. She'll still scream every time she sees Boris and Doris. Her mom will still call the pound if she sees us. It was dumb, but . . . it felt like the right thing to do."

Charlie smiled. "Sometimes that's the only

way you can tell if you did the right thing . . . if it feels right to you."

It did feel right and having such neat friends felt right, too.

"Tag. You're it." I swatted Morris on the rump and took off for the tree.

ABOUT THE AUTHOR

Since NIKKI WALLACE'S first children's book, *Stubby and the Puppy Pack*, lots of changes have occurred. Instead of living in the city, she and her husband Jon-Ed Moore are now next-door neighbors to her parents, Bill and Carol Wallace. Country life—with more space and no busy streets—has allowed their family to grow. They now have four dogs: Boris, Chancellor, Fitz, and Nilla.

Each of their pet's personalities has played a part in this second book about Stubby and her friends.